"I'm really sorry ab   said. "At least you can
say how lucky you are.

"I don't think I'm lucky. I think you are. I
would love to have a brother and a sister, no
matter what kinds of messes they made. Why
do you think I like coming to *your* house so
much? It's so quiet here, and there's nobody
to do anything with."

"If you had to live in my house for a week,
you'd go crazy,' I challenged.

"I would not, but you'd be bored silly here,"
she replied.

I sat back and thought for a minute.

"I wish we could," I said.

"Wish we could what?"

"Wish we could trade for a while."

"Trade what? Trade houses?" she asked

"Trade houses, trade lives, trade everything!"

"Hmmmm . . .," she replied as she mulled
the idea over. "You know, it's a neat idea.
Think our parents would ever go along with
it?"

"Probably not, but it would be fun!"

Oh, yeah?!

CHARITY & friends

$uper
Rich
$witch

by Deborah
Abrahamson

cover illustration by Aleta Jenks

To . . .
my husband, Joe, for his love,
never-ending support, and belief in my ability.
My wonderful children: Jen, Tim, Mike, and Becky,
for much-needed inspiration.

A special thanks for my mentor, fellow-writer,
and friend, Carol Perry, for her wonderful
encouragement and great advice.

⊿PAGES™

Second printing by Willowisp Press 1997.

Published by Willowisp Press
801 94th Avenue North, St. Petersburg, Florida 33702

Printed in the United States of America

2 4 6 8 10 9 7 5 3

ISBN 0-87406-855-X

One

"Hey, is that my favorite Charity in that tree? Are you collecting canned goods for the birds today, Charity?" asked a whiny voice from underneath the branches. I knew who it was before I even bothered to look down from the tree limb where I sat. Mickey the Creep is a pint-sized brat on an over-sized skateboard. He's like a gnat on a warm summer day—you can wave your hand to shoo it away, and a second later it's back. I've been stuck in the same class with Mickey every year since kindergarten . . . six years of seeing his round, freckley face everyday.

"Why don't you find someone else to bother?" I yelled down in annoyance.

"You know, Charity, with a name like yours, you should join the Red Cross," replied Mickey.

"Don't you ever get tired of those same old

5

stupid jokes?" I asked.

"Nope, I love my wonderful jokes," he said.

"Do me a big favor and get lost!" I replied, purposely dropping some leaves on his red-haired head.

"Adios, Señorita Charity." Mickey turned and skated away, still laughing.

Why did my parents give me a name like Charity? It's not a name—it's a place where you donate your old clothes.

I climbed down from the huge oak tree that's my favorite hide-out. I hopped on my bicycle and rode down to the drugstore on the corner to buy a Coke from the vending machine outside. As I leaned my bike against the wall, I could see my reflection in the store window. Straight, long brown hair, brown eyes, tall for my age, and kind of skinny—sometimes I don't think I look too bad. Most of the time, I think I'm ugly. My mother says most girls feel that way when they're twelve. She calls it "the awkward age." I hate that word—awkward—it sounds so geeky. Grown-ups know how to make you feel really stupid sometimes.

I drank my soda as I pedaled toward home, turning down the dirt rode that led to my house. My parents bought the old farm house when I was two years old. I can't remember ever living anywhere else.

I gulped down the rest of my Coke and buried it in the recycling bin outside. My mother doesn't like it when I drink soda. She's into health food—brown rice, tofu, stuff like that. We even grow our own vegetables.

I ran into the house where my mother was sitting cross-legged in front of a huge weaving loom. My mom enjoys weaving rugs. She sells them at craft festivals.

"Hi, Mom," I yelled, slamming the screen door. I wanted to make it into my room before my mother reminded me about my chores.

"Charity," she called.

"Too slow," I mumbled.

"I'd like you to take Shakespeare for a walk," she said, handing me the leash.

"Okay," I replied, feeling I got off easily. I whistled for the dog. Shakespeare, our huge white mixed-Labrador, came running. He was so excited, leaping up and down, I could hardly get the leash on him.

"Calm down, boy," I said as I was rewarded with a big slobbery kiss. "Yuck! I can't believe how big you've grown . . . you're still a puppy, and look at you."

"Oh, Charity," my mom went on, "pick up a newspaper on the way back. Your dad's article should be in it today." She handed me the money, and I zipped out the door.

My dad is a writer who specializes in articles about the environment. This particular article was a criticism of the new housing development. He felt that the people planning it weren't keeping enough trees and green space around it.

My parents are, as my father likes to say, "true children of the Sixties." That means that they believe in living as naturally as possible. We eat only organic vegetables, no chemicals or bug sprays on anything. Besides that, almost everything we buy is biodegradable—no aerosol sprays, no styrofoam, not much plastic. We use solar energy for heating our water, live in a house without air-conditioning, and ride our bikes for short trips. Living without air conditioning isn't easy in Florida—especially in the summer—but I'm used to it. Besides, our house is well-shaded by huge oak trees.

Shakespeare and I got to the end of our road. Instead of going our usual way, I decided to cut through the new housing development. It's called Summer Hill Estates. I think they're the prettiest homes in Lake Hills. Most of the houses were finished now. I love the sparkling new homes in all the latest colors. Thick green grass carpets the lawns and every bush is clipped into a perfect round ball. I pictured my own old wooden farmhouse with its front steps worn smooth from people going in and out for almost a hundred years.

Stopping for a second to tighten the band around my hair, I held the leash between my knees. Suddenly a silver-gray Persian cat stepped out from behind a bush. The cat saw Shakespeare and froze, but not soon enough. Shakespeare barked at the cat. The cat took off. Before I could get a firm grip on the leash, Shakespeare went bounding after it.

The cat raced for the open door of one of the houses. Our huge white Lab, with his leash trailing behind, looked as big as a horse galloping after the terrified cat. In desperation, I dove for the leash, practically landing on my nose on the front steps. I could feel my face burning with embarrassment as I looked up to see a pair of sneakers in front of my nose. I followed the shoes up, past the knees, into the glaring blue eyes of a girl about my own age.

Not knowing what else to say, I stammered, "I . . . I'm s-sorry. M-my dumb dog was chasing a cat."

The girl peered down at me. She had shiny blond hair that went just past her shoulders.

The designer T-shirt she was wearing was one that I'd been wanting for months. And I *knew* that I could have bought half of my back-to-school wardrobe for the cost of her sneakers alone.

"Well," the girl replied, "that just happened to be *my* cat."

I slowly stood up. In my "recycled" T-shirt and cut-off jeans, I felt like a little kid wearing play clothes.

"I . . . I'm really sorry," I said again.

"Well, I guess it's okay," she said and suddenly she started to laugh. "I've never seen that cat look so scared or run so fast!"

At that point, both of us began to laugh.

"You see," the girl explained, "Princess has lived her entire life indoors. She must have slipped out the open door when the new furniture was being delivered. She's never been nose-to-nose with a dog before." She started to laugh again. "My name is Brittany, what's yours?" she asked.

"My name is Charity," I replied.

"Charity," she repeated. "That's a cool name."

"You're the first person to think so."

"I can't believe that," she went on. "You should see what it's like to have a popular name like mine. Last year, there were two other Brittanies in my class. Talk about confusing. So, I guess you live around here, huh?"

Before I got a chance to answer, Brittany kept talking. "We just moved here from Atlanta. Where do you go to school?"

"I'll be starting at Lakeside Middle tomorrow," I answered.

"Oh, me, too," Brittany replied, "I'm so-o nervous about going to a new school. In Atlanta, I went to a private school, and we had to wear uniforms. I've had so much fun shopping for school clothes. I went to that store at the mall, The Taxi Cab. That's such a cool store, with the old taxi doors on the dressing rooms . . ."

While Brittany went on describing the clothes she'd bought, I was wishing that I could afford to buy *my* clothes at The Taxi Cab. It had to be one of the most exclusive stores at the mall. If I want expensive designer clothing, it means saving my allowance and baby-sitting money for what seems like forever.

"Does Lakeside Middle have a tennis team?" Brittany asked. "I played on the tennis team last year. Do you play?"

"I, uh, not that well . . .," I stammered.

"When we join the tennis club, I'll teach

11

you, if you'd like," she said, smiling.

Shakespeare was getting impatient and tugged at his leash.

"I'd better get going," I said, backing down the steps.

"Me, too," she replied, "We're still moving in. I'll look for you tomorrow." Brittany waved and started to shut the door.

I waved and turned to walk back the way I had come. As I walked, I realized that Brittany assumed that I lived in one of the new homes, not in an ancient farmhouse.

"Once she gets a look at my house, well . . . I won't be getting any more invitations to the tennis club, that's for sure," I said to Shakespeare as we jogged along. I wondered if I'd done the right thing. Maybe I should have told her right away that I don't live in Summer Hill.

"Oh, Shakespeare, what my mother says is true. I'm as awkward as they come!"

Two

I'm in a long dark hallway. I'm not sure where I am when suddenly I realize that this is my new school. Students are marching all around me. They are staring straight ahead like zombies. I don't know where to go. I turn to ask someone next to me. She looks at me as if I am speaking a foreign language and keeps on walking. All of them start walking faster and faster until they start running. The people are getting bigger, and all at once I'm surrounded by shoes . . . big, giant shoes. If I don't get out of the way, the shoes will step on me. Help!

I sat up in bed. Wow, what a nightmare!

The sun was just peeking in my bedroom window. It was time for me to get up. Today was Wednesday—the first day of school. It seemed really strange to be going to school

13

without my two best friends. And now on top of everything else, I don't know quite what to say if I happen to run into Brittany. No wonder I had that awful dream.

"I'll try not to think about it, " I decided as I finally got up. "After all, I don't even know if we're in the same grade."

After pulling nearly every outfit I own out of the closet, I picked out my favorite jeans and a soft teal-colored shirt. Looking at my reflection in the mirror, I actually felt pretty good about the way I looked.

I stepped into the hall and ran straight into one of my seven-year-old brother's beloved contraptions. Zachary had rigged a trip wire so that when I ran into it, his cap gun went off. The resulting explosion nearly sent me careening head-first down the stairs.

"M-o-m-m-m!" I yelled. "He's doing it again!"

From the foot of the stairs, my mother called out and confronted Zach.

"Zachary, how many times do I have to tell you? The staircase is not a place to play. Someone could get hurt."

"I wasn't playing," insisted Zach as he peeked through the railing. "I was inventing."

"Regardless," Mom continued, "get it out of here—NOW!"

14

Sighing loudly, Zach set to work, taking apart his latest creation. My brother, Zachary, is a certified genius. Even though he's only finished first grade, he enjoys reading encyclopedias, newspapers, just about anything. He loves to "invent" things, which has caused me all sorts of problems. Once he taped down the "talk" button on his walkie-talkie and hid it under my bed. Then, he listened to the conversation of my birthday-slumber party from the comfort of his room. He was having a great time, until our father discovered his little prank.

I went into the kitchen and sat down at the table between my dad and my little sister, Molly.

"Me cake! Me cake!" Molly squealed from her high chair.

"Okay, you cake," Dad said, putting a blueberry muffin on her tray. Molly's just two years old and seems to be learning a new word every day.

Dad was going over an article he'd written for his newsletter, *Earth News*. Just as the name suggests, all of the articles were about ecology and the environment. If he ever caught us wasting paper or leaving the water running, look out! Once when he saw me throw a gum wrapper out the car window, I got an hour-long lecture on pollution. The speech ended with an explanation about how it could cause the earth's temperature to rise until the polar ice caps melted. I worried about that for quite a while. I pictured myself waking up one morning to find my bed floating out to sea.

"Well," Dad said, "I've got to run. Tell me all about your first day when I get home tonight." After good-bye kisses all around, he was out the door.

Zach ambled up to the table and picked up a blueberry muffin. Examining it closely, he asked, "I wonder which part of the muffin digests faster, the bread part or the blueberries?"

"Mom-m-m," I wailed. "He's making me sick."

"Can we have a nice peaceful breakfast?" Mom asked. "Just once, please?"

We finished breakfast quietly. I said good-bye to everyone, and ran to the bus stop. While I waited, I looked over my schedule and tried to figure out where my classes were located. At New Student Orientation the counselors gave us a map of the school. Unfortunately, the way the classes were numbered made no sense at all. B-2 through B-9 were on one side of the main hall, B-29 was right across from them, but the other "B" classes were on the other side of the library. I felt like a human hamster about to be released into a maze.

"I'll be lost for days," I mumbled as I felt something land on my shoe.

"Here, Charity," bellowed an all-too-familiar voice. "It's my donation for today." Mickey the Creep and his buddies howled with laughter as I kicked the penny off my shoe in disgust. The bus arrived, and I decided to spend the ten minutes it took to get to the school trying to ignore them.

When I stepped off the bus at Lakeside Middle, I couldn't believe it. There was Brittany —getting out of a Mercedes. I took off in the opposite direction hoping to find my homeroom. So many kids were going in a zillion different directions. Incredibly, I actually found the right room number. Settling myself at an empty desk, I looked around to see if I recognized anyone. Nope, not a soul. My first two classes were the same way—I didn't know one single, solitary person.

By third period, I was just beginning to feel that I didn't have to worry about running into Brittany, when in she walked. Luckily for me, we were assigned seats at the opposite ends of the room. I spent the next hour trying to avoid looking her way. When the bell rang, I practically flew out of the room. I ran head-long into the first person I recognized all day, Heather the Brain.

"Where's the fire?" squawked Heather, pushing up the large glasses that were slipping down her nose.

"There's somebody I'm trying to avoid," I told her.

"That's what the boys usually say about me," Heather said sarcastically.

"Oh, Heather, they do not!" I laughed as we continued walking down the hall. It is true though that some of the kids think Heather is a nerd. She got the nickname "The Brain" because she is really smart and wears these big glasses. I think she's a nice person and she always makes me laugh.

As I sat in my next class, I realized that sooner or later I was going to have to talk to Brittany. No way was I going to be able to avoid her forever. By lunch time, I had convinced myself to relax a little. I didn't know anyone in the cafeteria, so I sat there alone. I felt kind of stupid, like I was at a party but I hadn't been invited. I finished eating and just sat there studying my schedule. When lunch was almost over, I looked up and there was Brittany.

"Hi, remember me?" she asked.

"Uh, ye-a-a-a-h, I, uh, sure," I stammered.

The bell rang signaling the end of lunch.

Brittany said, "Oh, no, too bad. I guess I have to run. Maybe we can eat lunch together tomorrow."

"Yeah, okay," I said, feeling relieved that I had been "saved by the bell."

I saw Brittany again later that day in gym class. She waved to me from the other side of the gym. The class was huge, and as soon as the bell rang, I had to run to my bus.

That night at dinner, my mom and dad wanted to hear how my first day went. "Did you get together with any of your friends from last year?" asked Dad.

"Not really," I answered, gloomily. "Kim and Linda got zoned for that other school, the one that just opened. I wish they were still here with me."

"Lakeside was getting overcrowded," Dad replied. "You'll make new friends."

"Easy for you to say," I said quietly.

"What did you say?" he asked.

"Oh, nothing," I said.

My mom was more sympathetic. "I know it's difficult to be twelve years old, new to a school, and minus your two best buddies. But you're such a likable person, Charity. You'll make lots of new friends. You'll see. Why some of my very best friends, I didn't even meet until I was in high school."

I got up from the table. "I've got books to cover, and homework to do . . .," I said. *I've also got a huge headache,* I thought. I went into the kitchen and got paper grocery bags and tape.

I dragged everything upstairs to my room and plopped down on my rug. As I covered my books, I thought about my weird first day. I decided to call Kim—I could tell her about my problem. I've known Kim since kindergarten. We've always been able to tell each other everything.

"Hi," I said when I heard Kim answer the phone.

"Oh, hi, Charity," she said. "We missed you today at school."

"Yeah, I missed you guys, too," I said.

"I love middle school," she said. "It was so cool . . . Linda and I have almost *all* our classes together. We couldn't believe how lucky we were. Oh, and remember Kurt, that really cute boy with those neat blue eyes?"

"Remember him?" I replied, feeling annoyed. "Of course, I remember him. It was only last year we were in the same class."

"Uh," Kim paused, "yeah, of course, well, he

sits right in front of me in three of my classes. Oh, wow, in the first class, he turned around and said 'hi' to me, and then after the second class, he walked me down the hall. He's so cute! Linda says she wants to have a party sometime and invite him. Oh, that would be so cool. Linda and I walked home today and we were planning what to wear tomorrow. Oh, and I forgot to tell you the school is so nice. My locker is right next to Linda's, so we can meet after school everyday."

I felt strangely left out, like what my dad calls "a fifth wheel." Somehow, I ended up not being able to tell Kim much of anything. By the time I hung up, I felt worse than ever.

Molly toddled in to say goodnight. I gave her a big hug and she smiled up at me.

"Oh, Molly," I said, "sometimes I wish I was little like you—no problems, just playing all day. You're so lucky. What should I do, Molly?" I stroked her baby-soft hair. "Well, one thing's for sure. No more hiding and running away. I want to make some new friends. As far as Brittany is concerned, I just won't say where I live. I'll just let her think I live in Summer Hill."

Three

"R-r-r-i-ing-g-g!" The lunchroom bell clanged. Boy, it's really loud when you're standing right underneath it. It was lunch time, and I was waiting just outside the cafeteria for Brittany. She'd stopped by my desk during class that morning and asked me to wait here for her. I just hoped it wouldn't be too difficult to pretend that I lived in Summer Hill.

Brittany walked in, and I waited while she bought her lunch.

"So you bring your lunch?" she asked as we sat down at one of the tables toward the back.

"Oh, absolutely," I said. "Cafeteria food is so-o gross!"

Brittany looked down at her tray and frowned a little.

"Sorry," I said. "I'll share some of my lunch with you if you'd like."

"Thanks" she said. "I think I'll bring my

own lunch tomorrow. So, anyway, what do you think of middle school?"

"Well," I said, "it's more confusing than I expected . . . and I hate having to look at that 'new student' map. You might as well wave a flag that says, 'I am a sixth grader.' This morning one of the older boys laughed at me, grabbed it out of my hand, and threw it in the garbage."

"Oh, wow, what'd you do?"

"I felt like a total geek, but I wasn't sure where my next class was . . . so I dug it up out of the garbage."

"How humiliating!" Brittany was sympathetic.

I nodded in agreement.

Brittany said, "I hate not knowing anyone."

"Me, too," I said offering her a cookie. "My two best friends ended up at the new middle school, so I understand exactly how you feel. I know a few people, like Heather, the one wearing glasses at the next table. She's really nice, and she's super-smart. But I don't have many classes with her because she's in all these really advanced subjects—like she's taking algebra already. I mean, I like her, but we don't seem to have too much in common. Anyway, you never told me why you moved here from Atlanta."

"My dad was offered a better job. Nobody asked me. He just came home from work one day and said, 'Guess what? We're moving.'"

"Just like that?"

"Yeah, just like that. I know it stinks, but what could I do?" She poked around with the food on her tray for a minute. Then she asked me, "Do you have any brothers or sisters?"

I nodded, "One brother and one sister. They're both younger than I am."

"You are so lucky," she said, "I'm an only."

"Oh, you wouldn't say that if you met my brother." I said, laughing.

"Why do you say that?" she asked.

"He's unbelievable. He spies on me and plays tricks on me all the time. He especially enjoys scaring me. I practically fell head-first down the stairs yesterday because of his so-called invention."

"Oh, no," Brittany said, and she started laughing. "It sounds like it's fun at your house. I'd love to be a big sister."

"My sister, Molly, is sweet, though. She's not much more than a baby, just learning to talk, and so cute—not at all like brat boy."

The bell was about to ring, so we got ready to leave. As we walked back to our classes after lunch, Brittany invited me to come over to her house and do homework after school.

"Well, I'd like to," I said, "but I'd have to call my mom first."

"No problem," Brittany replied. "My mom picks me up right after school. I'm sure she'll say it's okay, and we'll go call your mom. So what do you say?"

"Yeah, I guess it would be all right," I said. As I walked to my next class, I wondered if maybe I was pushing my luck by going over to Brittany's house already. Was it going to be impossible for me to avoid telling her where I really live? But I really wanted to go. I felt like Brittany was my life preserver, and middle school was the Pacific Ocean. I'd have to have a good excuse ready if she asked about coming to my house.

Brittany waited for me after school. After I called home to get the okay, we walked to her mom's car.

"Hi, I'm Brittany's mother," she introduced herself, "and you must be Charity. I'm happy to meet you. Brittany told me about you."

"H-h-hello," I said as I climbed into the car. I shut the door and we pulled away. During the drive, I couldn't keep my eyes off Brittany's mother's long gorgeous nails. They were perfect, with a beautiful design on each ring finger, and the diamonds . . . wow! Brittany and her mother talked about school.

In no time at all, we were pulling into their driveway.

As we stepped in the door, they told me to make myself at home. Nothing could have prepared me for the way that house looked— it belonged on the cover of a magazine. Everything was brand new. The tabletops gleamed and each piece of furniture in the room matched exactly. Even the flowers on the tables coordinated with the colors in the room. A baby grand piano sat in one corner, and I could see a big, formal dining room off to the side. I followed them into the kitchen.

Her mother said, "I'm still unpacking dishes, but if you both want a snack, you can use paper plates."

Brittany grabbed a few cookies and two sodas and led the way up the stairs to her room. If the downstairs was perfect, her bedroom was even more so. It was *everything* I ever wanted in a room. A huge, quilt-covered canopy bed was in the middle. A dresser and vanity was on one side. A large desk and computer was on the other. One entire wall was taken up by an entertainment center with a TV, VCR, stereo system, and video games. Beautiful porcelain dolls occupied a shelf above a cozy pillow-filled window seat. Everything was so immaculate, I was afraid to sit down.

Brittany solved the problem by tossing off her backpack and flopping down on the bed. I carefully sat on the other end.

"Well, I guess we'd better get the homework over with," Brittany said.

"Yeah," I said. "It's the first thing my mother will ask me about when I get home."

"You'd think they'd give us a break. It's only the second day of school," she said.

I nodded as she put on some music for us to listen to as we both got to work. Brittany pulled her math book out of her backpack and started on some problems, while I opened my Language Arts notebook. We worked quietly for a while.

"How long have you lived in Summer Hill?" Brittany finally asked.

I was right in the middle of writing a paragraph. Without even looking up, I replied absentmindedly, "M-mmm, quite a while . . . since I was about two."

"But I thought they only started building this development last year."

"Uh, no, I mean, we've lived in this town since I was two. We moved into Summer Hill last year. Did you get that assignment in third period?" I said quickly to change the subject.

"Sure," she answered as she searched

through her backpack for her assignment notebook.

As we continued our homework, I glanced over at Brittany. Did I do okay covering up my mistake? Did it sound kind of strange when I switched topics completely? She didn't seem to notice.

I looked around the beautiful room again and wondered whether she even realized how good she had it—her fantastic clothes, big house, perfect room. Probably not. I felt a little jealous.

"So your brother can be a problem sometimes?" Brittany asked.

"Sometimes? More like most of the time," I said. "You can't imagine what it's like living with this little junior scientist. His weird contraptions drive me crazy. One day he used his toy building sets to rig up a catapult. He sat in the garden, springing tomatoes into my room. What a mess!"

"Didn't he get in trouble?"

"Oh, yeah, he did. But you see, my parents say the problem is that even though he's as smart as someone much older, we have to remember that he's still just a little boy."

"Your family grows vegetables in your own garden? You must have a big yard. Where is your house?"

28

Little bells of warning began going off in my head. "I, uh, yeah, that was our old house." I changed topics again. "So, what do you think about the geography teacher . . . isn't she strange?"

"Boy, is she ever . . ." Brittany went on about the teacher while I breathed a sigh of relief at not being caught in my deception. As we sat there talking about school, I was feeling more and more nervous about everything. Finally, I felt like I couldn't sit still any longer.

"Brittany, I'm going to have to be getting home," I said suddenly.

"Oh, no, so soon?" Brittany looked disappointed.

"Yeah, uh, you see, I have to . . . uh . . . baby-sit. Yea, that's right, baby-sit," I said.

"Oh, okay," Brittany sounded puzzled. "Do you need a ride home? My mom won't mind, I'm sure."

"Oh, no, I'll just walk." I got my things together quickly. "I forgot that I promised to baby-sit, so I'll just run home. But I'll see you tomorrow, okay?"

Brittany followed me to the door, and I hurried down the front steps. "See you," she called.

As I walked toward home, I realized how lame my excuse for leaving must have sounded. It was going to be harder than I thought to pretend to live in Summer Hill.

Four

I took my time walking home. I didn't even notice my mother working in the garden. I walked right past her and didn't say a word.

"Charity, are you okay?"

I looked up and there she was.

"Yeah, I'm okay," I said as I walked toward the door.

"Then why do you look as if the world is about to come to an end?" she asked.

I didn't know what to say, so I just shrugged my shoulders and went inside. I climbed the stairs and went into my room. A few minutes later, my mother came in. Shakespeare followed her and greeted me with his tail wagging.

"Charity, are you feeling okay?"

"I'm fine, really. It's just been a long day," I said.

"Well, okay, come down and talk to me if

you want," she said, slipping off the gardening gloves. "I'm going to start dinner." She put her hand on my forehead as if she was convinced that I was sick. Then she went back downstairs. The dog sat down beside me on the floor and rested his head in my lap.

"What am I going to do, Shakespeare? I've really backed myself into a corner this time. I can't keep lying. She'll find out where I live and then she'll hate me for lying to her. Of course, she may hate me anyway when she sees my stupid old house. Why did I start this whole thing in the first place?" I patted the dog's head. He looked up at me, thumped his tail on the wooden floor, and gave me a sloppy kiss.

"You could never lie to anyone, could you, Shakespeare? Maybe I could learn something from you." I leaned back against my bed and closed my eyes while I scratched Shakespeare behind his ears. "I know what I'm going to have to do. There's no other way. Tomorrow I have to tell her, because the longer I wait, the worse it's going to get." Somehow deciding what I had to do, made me feel a little better already.

* * * * *

The next morning, I could hardly keep my mind on my class work. Finally, the bell rang for lunch. I waited for Brittany to catch up with me. She smiled and waved her lunch bag.

"See? I remembered to bring a lunch today," she said.

I smiled back, and then took a deep breath.

"I've got something to tell you," I said, as we sat down at an empty table.

"What about?" asked Brittany.

"About me," I replied. "You see, I haven't been completely honest with you." Brittany looked puzzled. I found it hard to look at her as I kept talking. "The thing is, I don't really live in Summer Hill."

"You *don't?*" she said. "Well, then why did you tell me you did?"

"I know it sounds stupid, but I wanted you to think I did because I live in a house that's very different from yours."

"How?" asked Brittany.

"Well, for one thing, it's old—it's an old farmhouse, not too far from where you live. That's why I was walking my dog there," I said.

"I don't understand," Brittany said. "Why didn't you just tell me?"

"Because . . .," I said, "I was afraid you

33

would think I was weird, especially after we met that first day. I practically fell on my face in front of you. And you . . . you had such a beautiful new house, and you just assumed I lived over there, too. It's stupid to lie. I realized it yesterday when we were doing our homework. That's why I left the way I did. I'm sorry . . . I know you probably hate me now. In fact, I wouldn't blame you if you never wanted to speak to me again." I felt really embarrassed—in fact, I almost felt like crying.

Brittany said, "I don't hate you, Charity. I'm glad you told me the truth."

"Really?" I replied.

"Yeah, really," she said, "I want us to be friends . . . and friends, well . . . they have to be honest with each other."

"You're so right," I said, nodding in agreement.

"I was the one who just assumed you lived in Summer Hill in the first place."

"I should have told you when I met you, and I'm sorry. I'm not a liar, Brittany. Really."

"Good," Brittany went on, "and I'm not a snob. You don't have to live any place special for me, Charity."

I felt as if a huge weight had just been lifted off my shoulders.

"So . . .," she asked, "exactly what do you mean by a 'farmhouse'? Do you live on a farm?"

"No," I answered." It was once a farm, but most of the land was sold off before we bought it. We only have a couple of acres."

"You said it was old—exactly how old *is* it?"

"Over a hundred years . . ."

"Wow!" she said. "It sounds cool. Can I come over and see it?"

"Uh, sure," I said, surprised that she really wanted to see it.

"How about if I come over today? It's Friday, so we don't have much homework. My mom can give us a ride to my house, and then we'll walk over to yours."

"Okay." I nodded as the bell rang signaling the end of lunch.

I felt so much happier the rest of the day. No more worrying about how I was going to tell Brittany about my house or about how long it would be before she found out where I lived.

After gym class, I waited for Brittany by the lockers. Her mom picked us up, and we rode to Brittany's house. We went inside and dropped off her backpack. Then we grabbed two Cokes from the refrigerator and told her mom that we decided to walk on over to my house.

As we got to the dirt road, Brittany could see the farmhouse and the garden.

"Charity, it really is neat! Wow, look how big your yard is—and look at the garden! We've never grown vegetables. In fact, we never grow anything. We've always had a gardener do all the work."

We walked up to the door. I couldn't believe that Brittany found all the old stuff so interesting, but she did. She loved our antique furniture and my mother's rugs. She loved the kitchen pantry with the different kinds of vegetables we'd canned ourselves. She kept wondering out loud about all the people who'd lived here through the years.

"Just think," she said, "people were probably born in this house—in fact, some probably died here, too."

"Yu-u-uck," I said.

"You're right," my mother answered as she walked into the kitchen. "I have a history of our house in my desk." My mother smiled. She seemed happy that someone was actually interested in her house. "You must be a new friend of Charity's."

"Mom, this is Brittany," I said. "She lives over in Summer Hill."

My mother said hello. I worried that she might make a face when I mentioned the new subdivision. But instead, she told Brittany that she'd be happy to share our home's history with her anytime. We went on up to my room.

"Well," I said, "here it is—tah-dah! No TV, no stereo, no video games, just a plain old bedroom. We do have a computer, but it's downstairs, 'cause it's my parents'."

"I like your antique bed."

"Yeah, the bed's as old as the house. My mother made the patchwork quilt. She wove the rug for me, too, before I was born."

"Wow, that's so cool," Brittany said bending down to touch the soft colors. "It's beautiful."

Just then, as if on cue, Zachary came flying into the room. He was dressed in his "world-famous detective" disguise, followed by Molly wearing a cowboy hat and Dad's boots.

"Oh, no," I said to Zachary in particular. "Why are you coming in here?"

Brittany started to laugh, "Oh, they are so cute! Who are you supposed to be?" she asked Zach.

"I am Sherlock Zachary Holmes," he said. "At your service." Then he looked at her closely through a magnifying glass. "Definitely a suspect. Fingerprint them, Watson," he said to Molly.

"Fing-primp-em," Molly repeated after him.

37

Sherlock Zachary turned his magnifying glass on Molly. "And you, Miss, are a suspect, too. Where did you get those boots?"

"MY boots!" Molly said loudly.

I noticed that Brittany was still laughing at them.

"They are so-o funny," she said.

"Oh, yeah, they're a laugh a minute," I replied sarcastically.

"You don't know how lucky you are," she said.

"That's funny, " I said. "I was thinking the same thing about you yesterday at your house."

"Really?"

"Yeah," I said. "You have everything—your house is so perfect . . . and your room, well, it's like my dream room."

"Well," she said, looking at Molly and Zach, "you've got the brother and sister I've always dreamed of having."

"Believe me," I replied, "you can have them . . . anytime!"

Five

That evening after Brittany went home, Dad called me to the table. Everyone else in the family was already there, waiting for me.

"I'm here," I answered, smiling, as I bounced into the kitchen.

"Well, someone looks happy," Dad remarked.

"Brittany and I had a good time," I said.

"She seems like a nice girl," Mom replied. "I guess you know her from school, right?"

"Yeah. Remember I called you before I went to her house the other day."

"Oh, that's right, now I remember . . . Summer Hill."

"Summer Hill . . . hmmmppphh," Dad added with a frown.

"Oh," I said, "you should see how beautiful her house is. Everything is new—the house,

39

the furniture. And her room. Wow! She has everything—a TV, VCR, video games, a computer. All her own, too."

"Wow, her own computer!" Zach the whizkid was excited at the idea of a private computer.

Molly clapped her hands and echoed Zach, "A puuuu-ter."

My father looked unimpressed.

"Well, she seemed to like this house quite a bit," my mother said proudly. "She was curious about the people who'd lived here through the years and wanted to know the history of the house."

Now, of course, my father looked impressed.

I had to agree that Brittany liked everything I showed her around here—she even liked my brother. I looked over at him as he slurped strings of spaghetti into his mouth and tried to balance a meatball on his fork.

"Glad she can't see you now," I mumbled, glaring at him.

The meatball bounced off his fork and landed in my lap.

"Oh, no!" I flopped the meatball onto the table, jumped up from my chair, and tried to wipe off the mess. "You little brat!"

"Charity!" Mom said. "It was an accident.

40

There's no reason to call him a brat."

"I think there's every reason. He pulls all these stupid little stunts and gets away with them. Look at my new jeans! I saved up my allowance and baby-sitting money for these. Brittany doesn't have to save her own money up, and she has designer everything. But then she doesn't have a bratty little brother around to ruin it!"

"I think we've heard quite enough, Charity!" Dad was practically yelling. "Go to your room. I don't want to hear another word out of you."

"Gladly," I said as I stomped up the stairs. "He can play with his food, drop it on my lap, and ruin my clothes, but I get sent to my room."

I was so mad. After I changed my jeans, I sat down in the middle of my room and imagined what I would do to Zach if I had the chance. I pictured a pile of spaghetti landing on his head and huge glops of tomato sauce dripping down and covering his face. Better yet, I would throw ten plates of spaghetti at him, or even a hundred. There was knock at the door.

It was Mom. "If you've calmed down sufficiently, I saved your dinner. But, first," she stepped aside, "someone has something he would like to say."

Zach stepped forward. "I'm sorry about your clothes." He looked genuinely worried.

"Oh, uh, okay," I stammered. "I guess it'll probably wash out." He gave me a little hug and ran back down the stairs.

A few minutes later, I went into the kitchen and sat down to eat. It was quiet and peaceful now. This is what it would be like to be an only child. Lucky Brittany.

After I finished eating, I brought the phone into my room and called her.

"You are so lucky," I told her. "My brother dropped food on my clothes at dinner tonight."

"He may seem like a pain to you," she said, "but I still think you're the lucky one. It's so quiet at my house sometimes. Besides, your brother and sister really are cute. You just don't see it because you're with them all the time. And you know what else? Your whole family sat down to dinner. A real dinner. Most of the time, my mother doesn't even cook. She'll be starting her new job next week, so we'll be going out to dinner, or Dad will bring home Chinese."

"Gee, I thought with that big kitchen that your mother loved to cook."

"Oh, she cooks on weekends when they entertain my Dad's business clients, or they'll make pancakes together on Saturday morn-

42

ings . . . or caterers will use the kitchen sometimes."

"Wow, caterers?"

"It's really not that big of a deal."

"Sure sounds like it is."

"Tomorrow's Saturday. Want to do anything?" Brittany asked.

"Sure," I said. "I know I'll get stuck working in the garden in the morning. But after that I can do something"

"Okay. Call me in the afternoon. My parents are forcing me to go to a play at the Arts Center, but that's not until evening."

"Well, I'll trade your play for the bugs in the garden any day."

"Not if you've been to as many boring plays as I have. I'll stop by your house tomorrow, okay?"

After saying good-bye, I just stayed there on the bed, thinking about things. I'd never known anyone whose life was so different from mine. First it's her house and her clothes and her parents, then it's catered dinners and going to plays. The only play I'd ever been to was Zach's. I watched him hop around as a frog two years ago in the kindergarten's "Welcome, Spring" recital.

And I could scarcely imagine what it was like to have a mother who didn't cook. Nobody to say, "Eat this and try that." Just order exactly what you feel like eating right then and there. I wondered whether the caterers dressed like the maids and butlers that you see on television. I bet they have candlelight dinners and everything. It was just like there was this whole other world out there, and it was just a couple of blocks away.

My mother tapped at the door even though it was open.

"You still awake?" she asked.

"Yeah, I was just talking to Brittany."

"That's nice. I just came up to ask you if you want me to spray some stain remover on those jeans. I'm sure the stain will wash out then."

"Okay, thanks . . .," I paused. "Mom, did you ever have friends who were really different from you?"

"Oh, sure. Still do, why?"

"It's just that Brittany's life is so unlike mine . . . it's just weird, that's all. I mean, I told you how her house is so beautiful and how she has everything. She's so lucky. She's an only child, too, so there's nobody to bug her or mess up her stuff."

"Oh, Charity, you know you'd miss Zach and Molly—"

I interrupted, "I'm not trying to get rid of

them . . . I just wish I was some place else sometimes."

I noticed my mother looked a little hurt at what I'd said.

"Well, you'd miss them if they weren't here. Goodnight, Charity," she added as she left the room.

Six

I overslept the next morning. Usually, Zach and Molly are running around on Saturdays, jumping on the beds, screaming, and chasing each other. But, for some reason, it was unusually quiet this morning.

I got up and slowly trudged down the stairs.

When I looked over at the table, I was surprised to see five people finishing breakfast.

"Well, hello, sleepyhead," Dad called when he saw me. "Look who joined us for breakfast this morning."

I rubbed my eyes thinking I was still half-asleep and must be dreaming.

"Hi!"

It was Brittany, looking for all the world like she belonged there, happily munching on a blueberry muffin.

"Hi," I said, self-consciously pulling down

46

the short nightshirt that I was wearing.

"Brittany came to the door this morning and we invited her to eat breakfast with us," Mom explained as she smiled over at Brittany.

"Especially since someone we know was still zonked out," Dad joked.

"And as you can see," Brittany said as she stood up, "I'm all dressed for garden duty."

Sure enough, Brittany had on cut-offs and a T-shirt.

"You mean you *want* to work in the garden?" I asked.

"I think it'll be cool," she replied.

"Well," Dad said, getting up from the table, "unless we want to get stuck working in the heat of the day, we'd better get started."

Shakespeare jumped up and down at the door to the yard, barking in anticipation.

Molly took Brittany's hand, "I show you my garden, Buu-wittany."

"It's not just your garden, Molly," Zach spoke up, taking Brittany's other hand and leading her outside.

"Charity," Mom said, "after you finish eating, I want you to do the rest of these dishes before you come join us." Then she and Dad walked out together.

So I sat down to breakfast alone while

Brittany accompanied my family to the garden. I finished eating, washed the dishes, and hurriedly dressed to go outside. It wasn't that I was in such a hurry to work in the garden, but I wanted to see Brittany out there with my own two eyes. Sure enough, there she was, standing next to my father. He was obviously in his glory as he explained to her the benefits of organic gardening.

"Most people just don't realize how much pesticide is sprayed on the produce you buy in the market, but these . . .," he said as he picked a red, ripe tomato from the vine, "these are all chemical-free."

He handed the tomato to Brittany as if it were made of gold.

Brittany examined the tomato and nodded.

"Neat," she said.

"Are you giving her a lecture, Dad?" I asked, rolling my eyes at Brittany.

"No, Charity, it's not a lecture if your friend is interested," he answered defensively.

"I think it's fascinating," Brittany said.

"One of the simpler ways to get rid of pests is to just pick them off." Dad demonstrated as he pulled off a large beetle and dropped it into a jar.

Surely Brittany would run from the garden screaming at the mere suggestion of touching bugs—or so I thought. But Brittany actually reached over and plucked a bug off as if she'd been doing it her whole life. I was absolutely speechless. This girl who lived in luxury was pulling bugs off of the plants growing in my backyard. It was just too weird.

I got to work and pulled some weeds. Then I helped my mother harvest some of the vegetables that were ready to be picked, while Brittany happily learned about the joys of composting. In a couple of hours, we were finished, just as the sun was beginning to get hot.

Brittany and I sat down on the shady front porch and drank some lemonade.

"Pheeeww," she said as she wiped her forehead, "that's hot work. Makes you appreciate what it must be like to be a farmer. I feel like going for a swim. Want to grab your swimsuit and go with me? We can use the pool at the tennis club."

"Sure," I nodded, "give me about five minutes."

After I cleaned up and got the okay, Brittany and I headed over to her house.

We walked along quietly for a few minutes, until finally she spoke up.

"You are so lucky," she said.

"Me?" I said with total disbelief.

"Yes, you. You have such an interesting family. They're, I don't know, I guess they're creative. I mean your mom weaves and paints. Your dad writes and gardens and knows so much about the environment. My parents wouldn't know the first thing about any of that."

"So," I answered, "do you think my parents would know anything about plays and catered dinner parties or entertaining business clients? They're just so different."

"Like night and day," she agreed.

* * * * *

Brittany and I had a good time at the pool. She bought me lunch, which we ate poolside. We swam and raced each other. She showed me some of the fancier dives she knew from taking diving lessons. It was pretty hysterical when I tried them for the first time and ended up doing a belly flop.

"Oh, no," Brittany said, glancing at her watch. "I'm in trouble now. I was supposed to have been home half an hour ago. I have to get dressed up for that play."

We quickly got our things together and showered off in the club locker room. Then we hurried the couple of blocks to Brittany's house. Her mother was waiting for us at the door.

As we walked up the sidewalk, Brittany leaned over to me and quietly said, "Uh-oh, not a good sign . . ."

"Do you know what time it is, young lady?"

"I know, I know," Brittany answered. "I'll hurry up now and get done. Come on up with me, Charity, while I get ready."

Her mother didn't seem to object so I followed her to her room.

I sat on the bed while Brittany blow-dried her hair. Then she put on a beautiful forest-green, semi-formal dress. I helped her pull her hair up and we clipped on a matching green bow. She looked so grown-up, like she was going to a prom.

"Brittany," I said, "I have never seen anyone our age with a dress like that."

"I like the dress, but I really hate going to these plays."

There was a knock at the door. "Can I come in?" asked her father.

"Yes," she answered.

When he opened the door, I saw that he was wearing a tuxedo. I don't think my dad even wore a tuxedo to his wedding.

"Hello," he said to me, "you must be Brittany's friend. She told us about you."

I nodded. "Hello, I'm Charity." I felt my face flush. The thought of them discussing me was a little embarrassing.

"Well, Brittany, you look lovely. Hurry up, we're leaving soon. Nice meeting you, Charity," he added as he closed the door.

I told her, "I'd better go. Call me tomorrow."

She followed me as I walked down the stairs.

"Yeah, if I make it through tonight," she said sarcastically.

"You don't know how lucky you are. I would love to go to a play," I said.

Brittany's mother was waiting at the bottom of the stairs. She obviously heard what I said because she replied to me, half-kiddingly, "Maybe you should go next time instead of Brittany."

I smiled, a little embarrassed, and said, "Have fun," as I left to go home.

I walked through Summer Hill and then turned down my street until I got to my own long driveway. I could see my parents in the yard. My dad wore a short-sleeved plaid shirt, jeans, and a tattered straw hat. He was watering some of the plants in the garden. My mom pulled Molly and Zach around the yard in a little red wagon. She had on a pair of baggy overalls and was barefooted. I compared them in my mind to what Brittany's parents looked like as they left for the evening.

"It's so true," I said softly. "Just like night and day . . ."

Seven

The next week was a flurry of school activities. Everything was being set up for the new year.

Tuesday was Open House at Lakeside Middle. Each student and his or her parents had to follow the student's individual schedule to the various rooms and meet each of the teachers. When the bell rang for first period, we went to Language Arts. At least I got to start the day in a subject I like.

Miss Reynolds was a very young teacher, and she was fun. Second period I had Mr. Henry for Math. He wasn't bad. Then the bell rang for third period. The teacher was Mr. Boris. (We called him Mr. Boring.) All of the students and their parents went in and sat down. Mr. Boris spoke in a solemn monotone about the requirements of Earth Science. It was not exactly captivating. Brittany gave a little wave to me from across the room. When the bell signaled the end, we all met outside the classroom. Because this was normally our lunch time, we had a few free minutes.

"Mom, Dad," Brittany began, "these are Charity's parents."

"Hello, I'm Bill McKay, and this is my wife Carol," my father introduced himself as they shook hands.

"Tom and Candy Wilson. Nice to meet you. Our daughters seem to have become good friends."

"I always hate introductions," I whispered to Brittany.

"Me, too," she replied.

So we let our parents continue their conversation alone while we walked around. I couldn't stand listening. It was just too embarrassing. What if my father started telling them all about our "environmentally friendly" way of life? By the time he'd be finished, Brittany's parents would be wondering whether or not we had indoor plumbing. I was happy when the next bell forced them to go their separate ways.

The next class was a favorite of mine, too. I loved going to Fine Arts. Only it wasn't because I loved the art and music. It was because David Prince sat next to me in the class. I thought David Prince was the cutest boy in the whole school. He was tall and handsome, with brown eyes and shiny, blond hair cut in a surfer style.

So many students and parents turned up at this particular Open House that the teacher asked the kids if they wouldn't mind letting their parents have the chairs. I didn't mind at all. Especially when I had to sit on the floor . . . right next to you-know-who! All too soon, the bell rang again.

Next we went on to Reading. Then, finally, Gym., the other class I shared with Brittany. Because Open House always takes longer than expected, it was very late by the time we got finished. So I waved good-bye to her and my parents and I hurried home.

Wednesday was just a usual day, but Thursday was the school's first PTA meeting. Both of my parents went while I baby-sat Zach and Molly.

I read Molly a bedtime story and tucked her in early. Zach played math games on the computer until it was time for him to go to bed. Shakespeare kept me company while I did my homework. It didn't seem long before I heard the car pull in the driveway.

"We met Brittany's parents again at the meeting tonight," my mother said as she came in the door.

I looked up from the chapter I had just finished studying for tomorrow's quiz. The dog bounded over to them, his tail wagging with enthusiasm.

"They seem like very nice people," Dad continued where Mom left off. "They have a lot of good ideas for the school. You look surprised, Charity. Are you surprised about something?"

"I guess I figured that you probably wouldn't get along," I answered.

"Why is that?"

"You're so different."

"Not different in wanting the best education for our children. We're going to be working on a committee together for the next couple of weeks."

Somehow the thought of my parents and Brittany's working together was not very reassuring.

The next day in science, Mr. Boris assigned a project on the environment. We were allowed to choose someone to work with, so naturally Brittany and I picked each other. We had to make a poster that explained several different types of recycling and showed examples.

"Easy," Brittany said, "we'll go over to your

house and do it. Your family does so much recycling, it'll be a snap."

That afternoon, we arrived at my house carrying a big piece of poster board. We went out into the sunroom where we have a huge worktable set up. The table was covered with jars of paint that Zach had been using earlier. He had been decorating empty cardboard boxes to look like a town for his toy little people.

"Where do we begin?" Brittany asked.

"First, I guess we move all this junk," I said as I put the boxes and paints on the floor.

"Let's do what they call 'brainstorming' and just think of lots of ideas," Brittany suggested.

For about the next hour, we sat and wrote down all kinds of ideas. We decided to make our poster 3-D by gluing actual recycled products on it. We collected several examples from the different bins in my house. We even glued an apple slice on it as an example of recycling food materials into compost. We worked for a long time. Brittany was very good at organizing the material on the board so it looked attractive.

"I think it looks fantastic," I said as I stepped back to admire it.

"I think so, too," Brittany agreed.

"I'm starved. Want to see if you can stay for dinner?"

"That'd be neat. Whatever your mother is cooking smells great."

After my mother agreed, Brittany and I helped her finish making dinner. Then we set the table and made iced tea.

We all sat down, except for Dad, who was working a little late. I glared at Zach, just daring him to misbehave. He seemed very quiet, almost like he was worried about something. We were having homemade vegetable soup and freshly baked bread.

"This is delicious," Brittany said as she tasted the soup. "I can't believe you bake your own bread."

"Oh, it's not that difficult," my mother modestly replied. "Once you've made it a few times, you can do it with your eyes shut. It just takes time and a little planning."

"I wish I could learn to do it," Brittany said.

"Be happy to show you sometime," my mom answered.

After we'd all been eating for a while, Mom looked over at Zach.

"Aren't you feeling well, dear? You're hardly touching your food," she said with concern.

Molly pointed at Zach. "Zach, me pu-waint, uh-huh, we did," she nodded.

59

I didn't really understand what she was saying.

"Huh?"

"Me pu-waint. Me, Zach, we pu-waint."

"What are you telling us, Molly?" I asked. "Pu-waint? What's pu-waint?" I looked at Molly's arms. It looked as if she had some paint on her elbows. Suddenly, I understood. "Oh, no! Paint. She said *paint*, get it? Oh, no, they didn't . . .," I jumped up and ran into the sunroom. "Oh, no, they did . . . they painted our poster!"

By now everyone had followed me into the sunroom. Everyone that is, except Zach, who stood with his head bowed in the doorway. The poster that we had worked on so long and hard was covered with every possible color of paint.

"My goodness," Mom said, "Zach, why did you do this? You should know better. I can see how Molly wouldn't understand what she was doing, but you?"

Zach walked over to her and spoke quietly, "Molly did most of it. I just tried to make it look better. I tried to clean her up as much as I could, too. I'm sorry."

"Sorry!" I yelled. "Yes, you are sorry . . . a sorry excuse for a brother."

"Charity, there's no need to say something

like that. He told you Molly did it," Mom replied, trying to calm me down. "How did these paints get where Molly could reach them anyway?"

"I left them up high on the table, Mom, just like you told me," Zach said.

"I put them on the floor when we needed room to work on the table," I answered.

"Well, you could have prevented this from happening in the first place if you'd put the paints in the cabinet instead of on the floor. You know we have a two-year-old in the house, Charity. We all have to think of things like that. What if she had eaten some of the paint?"

"Oh, I guess it's my fault then," I said indignantly.

"It's not that it's your fault, but she doesn't know to stay out of this stuff."

"So I suppose that makes it okay then. It's just like everything else around here. They ruin it . . . ruin it all! Come on, Brittany, let's get our stuff together and go to your house. At least there we can do our project without having it messed up."

We got our stuff together, collected new examples, threw the painted poster in the trash, and left for Brittany's house.

Once we got there, we set up our work area

in the kitchen. It was very quiet in the house. Brittany's parents were in their family room, watching the evening news. Best of all, no one bothered us, unless you counted the time her cat tried to sit down in the middle of the paper.

"I'm really sorry about what Molly did," I said.

"She didn't mean it, Charity," she answered. "She's just too little to know better."

"Well, at least you can see now why I always say how lucky you are."

"I don't think I'm lucky. I think you are. I would love to have a brother and a sister, no matter what kinds of messes they made.

Why do you think I like coming to your house so much? It's so quiet over here, and there's nobody to do anything with."

"If you had to live in my house for a week, you'd go crazy," I challenged.

"I would not, but you'd be bored silly here," she replied.

I sat back and thought for a minute.

"I wish we could," I said.

"Wish we could what?"

"Wish we could trade for a while."

"Trade what? Houses?" she asked.

"Trade houses, trade lives, trade everything!"

"Hmmmm . . .," she replied as she mulled the idea over. "You know, it's a neat idea. Think our parents would ever go along with it?"

"Probably not, but it would be fun."

Eight

I knew it was weird. But once the subject of the two of us switching places was brought up, I could never quite get it out of my mind. For a whole week, all I thought about was how neat it would be.

It was especially hard for me when Zach did something stupid. Then I found myself wishing that I lived at Brittany's house.

Brittany seemed to be spending a lot of time thinking about it, too. Every day for a week, the subject dominated our conversations.

At school, we talked about it over lunch.

At home, we talked about it over the phone.

It was driving us crazy.

Unfortunately, in the process, we were driving our parents crazy, too.

"Brittany is so lucky," I announced as my family and I finished dinner Friday night.

"Here we go again," my dad commented, shaking his head in disgust.

"But, Dad, she *is* lucky," I said. "Her parents took her to an Ice Show last night."

"What's an Ice Show?" Zach interrupted.

"It's a show where fabulous, famous ice skaters figure skate and dance on the ice," I answered.

Zach jumped up from the table and announced, "Hey, look at me, Molly. I'm an ice skater." Then he pulled off his sneakers and slid across the wooden floor of the dining room in his socks.

Molly squealed with delight.

"Me wanna skwate, too," she said.

I couldn't stand it. Nobody was saying anything to make him quit. I got up and left.

I had to talk to Brittany.

". . . then he gets up and skates around the dining room in his socks," I said, explaining what happened.

Brittany laughed.

"Why are you laughing?" I asked. "It was really annoying."

"I can't help it," she said. "I could just picture Zach doing something like that."

"You wouldn't laugh if you had to live with that kind of stuff happening every day."

"Oh, yes, I would."

"Believe me, you wouldn't," I insisted.

"So here we are," Brittany replied, "everything just the same as it was before."

"Yeah," I said. "You with your quiet house. And me with my wacky brother! What I wouldn't give to be at your house right now."

"You know, if we want to switch so much, maybe we should just go ahead and ask our parents."

"They'll never go along with it," I said.

"All they can say is 'no.' How will we ever know if we don't try?" she answered.

"I guess you're right," I said.

"So does that mean you're going to ask your parents?" Brittany asked.

"I'll ask my parents if you ask yours," I agreed. "Like you said, all they can say is 'no.'"

I didn't know how to exactly bring up the subject of switching places. "You know, Brittany," I said, "I can't really walk up to my parents and say, 'Hey, Mom, Dad, I think I'll go over to Brittany's house and live for a while. See ya!'"

"We have to be tactful," she suggested.

"And we have to ask at the same time," I added. "I'm not exactly sure how to do it, though—maybe by talking to them about how they felt when they were our age."

"Good idea."

So we agreed that the next day, Saturday, was the day.

* * * * *

When I woke up the next morning, it was raining. That meant no working in the garden. Dad made us what he calls his "lazy-day" breakfast—pancakes with strawberry topping. After that, Mom and I helped clean up the kitchen. The rain wasn't letting up, so the day had all the signs of being totally dull.

I figured that now was as good a time as any to talk to someone. I decided that I'd try my mom first.

"Hey, Mom," I said as I sat down next to her at the table where she was painting.

"Hi, Sweetie," she said.

"Mom," I began, "did you ever want to live a different life from the one you have?"

"No, I wouldn't change a thing. I love my life. Except maybe I'd have a little more money. I think most people would like more money. But other than that, no, I wouldn't trade you guys for anything."

This wasn't going the way I'd hoped. I tried again.

"Well, maybe not now, 'cause you're grown-up and married. I mean when you were younger, like me. When you were my age, did you ever wish that your life could be changed, or somehow be opposite from the way it was?"

She stopped painting and gazed off into space.

Then she spoke wistfully. "Well, uh, yes, I guess when I was your age I did occasionally wish my that I had a more unusual life. I remember when we all went to see the circus. There was this whole family that did an act on the trapeze. They had a little girl who was about my age who performed with them. I remember wishing that I could be the little girl in that family. I thought it would be fantastic to be able to wear sparkling jeweled leotards and to do an act in the circus. Traveling from town to town, seeing the world. But, of course, now I think it would have been a terrible life."

"Why would it have been terrible? I think it sounds wonderful."

"Because," she frowned slightly, "that poor little girl didn't ever have any kind of a normal life. She didn't get to go to a regular school or have friends her age. Hers would have been a show-business kind of life, and that's not so great for a child."

"Well, I can see why that wouldn't be so good," I agreed. " But what about a more ordinary life—only different. Like sometimes

I wish my life was more like Brittany's."

"I can see why you would wish for something like that."

"You can?" I replied, getting excited at the idea that she might understand.

"Yes," she repeated, "I can. I mean you told us how she has a beautiful house and the perfect room. If I was your age, I'd wish for all those things, too."

"But you know what's weird?" I continued.

"What?"

"She wishes that she had a life more like mine."

"Oh, really. I guess you find that just incredible—that someone could possibly want a life like yours."

Uh-oh, I was losing her.

"No, it's not that it's incredible. It's just that the other day we thought it would be fun to switch."

My mother laughed. Then she realized that I wasn't kidding.

"You're serious, aren't you?" she said.

"Well, what's wrong with that?"

"Charity, I can't believe that you'd want to leave."

"Well," I answered, "it's not like I want to leave forever. Just for a while."

My mother didn't answer. She just shook

her head and went back to her painting.

I gave up for the time being and went out on the porch. Dad was sitting out there on the swing, listening to the rain drum on the tin roof. He rested one hand on Shakespeare who was sitting beside him. I wondered how I could bring up the subject to him. I really didn't want to be stuck here on a rainy day with both of my parents mad at me.

"Hey, Dad," I said as I sat down on the top step.

"Hi, Honey, what are you up to?" he asked.

"Oh, nothing. When do you think it'll stop raining?"

"Well, the weather says by this afternoon. There's supposed to be an early cold front. Might have record lows tomorrow morning."

I took a deep breath. "I was just talking to Mom about when she was my age."

"Hope you didn't make her feel like she was born back in the Stone Age."

"No, I was just curious about if she ever wished that her life was different."

"You mean extraordinary in some way?"

"Yeah, you know, when she was still a kid. Did you ever wish your life was different?" I asked.

"Well, sure," he said. "I think it's normal to be curious about other people and wonder

70

what it would be like to live their lives."

"Really?"

"Yes, when I was a boy I used to wish I could be a cowboy, an explorer, even a pirate."

"Well, I meant did you ever wish that you could be someone you knew, your own age?"

"Yeah, I guess I did. I once wished I was Colby Jackson. He was the richest boy in town. His father was the bank president, and his parents gave him anything and everything he ever wanted. I'm glad now that I wasn't him, though."

"Why?"

"He ended up in prison for stealing money from the bank."

I shrugged. Great—this isn't working either.

"Lately I've been wishing that I could live another life," I said, trying a slightly different approach.

"Oh, yeah? Whose life have you been wishing for?"

"Brittany's."

"I'm not really surprised," he said.

"No?" I replied. "Why?"

"You've been talking about her all the time lately—her house, her room with the TV and computer."

"But it's not just the things that she has, Dad. It's the fact that she's an only child and

71

she gets to do all kinds of special things. Things I'll never get to do. And you know what's funny? She wishes that her life was more like mine."

He chuckled a little. "She certainly seemed to have a good time last weekend."

"We even had an idea. You'll probably think it's crazy. But we thought that maybe we could switch lives for a while."

"Hmmmm . . .," he thought about that for a couple of minutes. Then he got up to go back in the house. "Interesting idea," was all he said.

I ran up to my room and called Brittany.

"So did you have any luck?" I asked.

"A little," she replied. "First my dad just laughed, then he looked kind of hurt."

"Yeah, I know what you mean. Only my mother looked hurt. She said she couldn't believe I was serious."

"I did better with my mom," she went on. "I just came out and told her that we wanted to switch places for a while. She looked surprised and said she didn't believe me. But then I told her to ask your parents tonight when they have their PTA fundraising dinner. I told her to see if we haven't really been talking about it. Then she said okay, she'd ask them."

"Well, just because she asks them, doesn't

mean they'll go along with it."

"True," Brittany answered, "but then my mother said, 'At least Charity might enjoy going to the theater with us.' Only I think she meant it sarcastically."

"My dad did just the opposite," I said.

"Of course, the night and day people, remember?"

"Yeah. He said it was an interesting idea."

"Well," Brittany said, "I guess we wait and see if they talk it over tonight."

* * * * *

That evening Brittany came over to help me baby-sit while our parents all went to the dinner. Both of us were so worried about what their answer was going to be that we could scarcely sit still. We played games with Molly and Zach. Then we tucked them into bed, and they were fast asleep by the time our parents returned.

When we heard the car in the driveway, we were so anxious that we ran into the kitchen. We wanted to see the expressions on our parents' faces when they came in. Would they look angry? Upset?

First, my mother came in, followed by Mrs. Wilson. Then Dad held the door for Mr. Wilson. They all looked the way they normally do.

"How did it go?" my dad asked.

We both answered, "Fine."

"I can see by the way that you're staring at us that you're wondering what we discussed tonight, aren't you?" Mr. Wilson asked.

We both nodded.

"Well," my father began, "Brittany's mother said that you wanted us to talk and see if you were both serious about switching places . . ."

"So we did, and we compared what you've both been saying," Mrs. Wilson continued.

". . . and the way you've both been acting," Mr. Wilson interrupted.

"At first, I was totally against this whole idea," my mother started to say, "but then as we talked I realized that you were both curious and maybe a bit envious of each other's lives."

"And in talking we even brought up the fact that exchange students travel to other countries to experience another way of life," Mr. Wilson explained.

"So I guess you can think of it as a 'mini-exchange' program," my dad said, "because we've decided that as long as you both follow some rules, we'll let you try switching homes. For two weeks, tops."

Brittany and I both jumped up and did a little cheer.

"Now, just hold on a minute. We wrote

74

down some rules and we want you to read them," Mom insisted.

". . . and then if you still want to go on with it, you both sign it," said Mrs. Wilson.

I took the sheet of paper from my father, and Brittany and I both read it.

Ground Rules for the Big Switch

1. *You must follow the rules of the family in whose home you are residing. The switch must be complete and authentic.*
2. *You must see or call your parents every day, just to let them know how you are doing and that every thing is okay.*
3. *The switch will last for a period of two weeks, starting tomorrow.*
4. *If at any time either of you decide that you need to return to your own home, the experiment is over and you will both do so immediately and without complaints.*
5. *We, the parents, may change our minds if unforeseen problems arise. There will be no argument if this occurs.*

"Wow, this sounds like a contract," Brittany commented.

"It is," her father replied.

"If you still want to do this," my mother

said, "you both need to sign it at the bottom."

"Exactly what does that mean, 'the switch must be complete and authentic'?" I asked.

"It means you can't have it both ways," my mom replied.

"In other words, you can't pick and choose what you like from each family," Dad went on. "You have to go by their family's rules, bedtimes, food preferences . . . whatever."

Brittany looked me.

"Doesn't sound like it'll be too tough," she said.

"Well, this was what we wanted," I said as I picked up the pen. "Let's go for it."

"Okay," Brittany replied. "Let's do it."

Nine

I thought it was all going to be so easy, but problems came up right away the next morning. The first one occurred when Brittany started to pack. She couldn't decide what to bring and what not to bring. She ended up packing half her room. She had about ten boxes filled with her stereo, CDs, telephone—anything she could haul. Her mother put a stop to that in no time.

"Just pack some of your clothing and personal supplies in a couple of suitcases. You wanted to see what it was like to live Charity's life," she said. "Remember, the switch is to be complete and authentic."

"Oh, yeah." Brittany shrugged and reluctantly agreed.

So Brittany had to spend half of the first morning unpacking.

I had a whole different set of problems.

77

I had to contend with Zach. I never ever believed it could happen, but he was actually quite upset that I was leaving.

"I don't want you to go away," he said tearfully, sounding like the sweetest little brother in the whole world.

"I'm not going away," I told him as I put my arms around him. "I'm just going to stay at Brittany's house, and only for a couple of weeks. Besides, I'll come to see you. But do you know what else? While I'm over there, Brittany's going to stay here in my room."

When I told him that he wiped the tears and his face brightened. Then he smiled a little and said, "I guess that might be fun." So much for being missed.

Once I got through all that, it took me a while to pack. I wanted to make sure that I had everything I needed, especially any dressy clothes that I might want to wear if we were going out. I was so excited. Just the possibility that I could be going to the theater was fantastic.

I carried the heavy suitcases downstairs where everyone was lined up like I was leaving for college.

"Bye, Mom," I said as I hugged her tight.

"Bye, Honey. You remember to call."

"I will. Remember, Zach, it's going to be fun."

Zach gave a slight smile.

Little Molly just said, "Bye-bye, Cha-witty."

Dad helped me load the suitcases into the car and off we went.

When I got to Brittany's house, her mother met me at the door and told me to make myself at home. Then she went upstairs to tell Brittany that my father was here to take her back to my house.

We met on the stairs. She was carrying two suitcases down. I was carrying two suitcases up.

"Well, I guess this is it," she said.

"Yeah, this is it. Call me later," I said.

"Oh, I will," she answered.

As soon as I opened the door to her room, I felt kind of strange. I felt like I was doing something wrong . . . like I wasn't supposed to be there all alone. It was just weird. But then I reminded myself that for the next two weeks, this was *my* room.

I put down the suitcases and sat on the bed. It was much bigger than my little antique bed at home. I stretched out on the thick, soft quilt and looked up at the lacy canopy. I closed my eyes for a minute.

It was so silent in the house. Complete peace and quiet for two weeks. Poor Brittany doesn't know what she's in for. Zach will run all around the place, in and out of her room. He'll tease Molly until she screams. Shakespeare will bark and chase them around. Yeah, I really got the best part of the deal. Wow, it was so calm and peaceful. I listened. I don't think I've ever been in a house that was this quiet. No sound . . . nothing at all. After a while, I heard a clock chime downstairs, then absolute silence again. In fact, it was almost too quiet. Finally, I couldn't stand it anymore. I got back up, went over to the stereo, and put some music on.

There, that was better. It was just going to take some getting used to.

The phone rang and I knew that it was most likely going to be Brittany before I even picked it up.

"Hi," she said.

"Hi," I said. I felt awkward.

"Well, I'm all settled in over here. I'm playing a game with Zach. What are you doing?"

"Not much yet."

There was a knock at the door.

"Hold on a minute, Brittany, someone's knocking at your . . . er, I mean, *my* door."

I opened the door. It was Mr. and Mrs. Wilson.

"I know this is last-minute, but we got so involved with this that we almost forgot completely about it. We have three tickets for today's football game. Think you can hurry up and get ready?" Mrs. Wilson asked.

'You mean, a real football game?" I asked in awe.

"Yes, *real* pro NFL football," Mr. Wilson added. "The Steelers were in the Super Bowl last year. They'll probably beat the Jaguars since they're fairly new, but it should be a great game. My boss gave the tickets to me to welcome us to the area. They're fabulous seats, right on the fifty-yard line. I hope you don't mind the short notice. It'll take us a couple of hours to get to the stadium."

"Mind? I can't wait. I'll be ready in two minutes."

Mr. and Mrs. Wilson left so I could get ready.

I opened my suitcase to find something to wear. Then I remembered that Brittany was still waiting on the phone.

"Geez, it took you long enough," she said when I got back to the phone.

"Sorry. I've got to go now anyway. Your parents just said that we're going to the football game today."

"Oh, that's right," she said. "I remember. Last week Dad mentioned that his boss gave him tickets to the game. I forgot about that.

Guess I can't go along, too, can I? Especially since there's only three tickets." She sounded almost annoyed.

"Guess not," I replied. "Well, I'd better go." I didn't want to waste any time on the phone now.

"Have a good time," she said. I could hear Zach and Molly yelling and Shakespeare barking in the background.

"Oh, I will," I said happily. "Believe me, I will."

Ten

I couldn't believe that I was really going to a professional football game. The first thing I noticed was the size of the stadium. It was absolutely huge. We showed our tickets at the turnstile to get inside the gate, then climbed the ramps that took us up to our level. After we showed our tickets a second time to a man at the entrance to our area, we were allowed to go to our seats. The game was about to begin, and we stood for the National Anthem.

Then, it was kickoff time. The Jaguars made a touchdown. The cheerleaders cheered. The crowd did the wave. Then the Steelers made a touchdown. Mr. Wilson was a Steelers' fan. He cheered and yelled. Then the Jaguars had the ball again. But the Steelers intercepted the ball and got another touchdown. The Steelers' fans went wild. Just before halftime, the Jaguars managed a field goal. The score was Steelers 14, Jaguars 10. A close game so far.

It was half-time before we knew it. Because we'd been in a hurry to get to the game, we didn't eat lunch before we left. Now we were all starving. Brittany's dad and I walked to the concession stand. We got pizza and soft drinks enough for all three of us. I was still hungry, so I went back for French fries. After that, a vendor came by with hot dogs. Boy, they sure looked good. So I bought one of those, too. Then, a kid sat down in front of me with cotton candy. Mmmmm . . . I just had to get some cotton candy—and, of course, another soda to wash it all down.

"You certainly have a healthy appetite for a slender girl," Mrs. Wilson commented as I devoured a big swirl of fluffy cotton candy.

Half-time was over and the game was about to begin again. I was sipping on the soda, when suddenly everything I'd eaten seemed to hit bottom. I felt like I was going to be sick. I guess I'd gone totally overboard on the normally forbidden junk food.

I mustn't have looked too well, either.

"Are you all right, Charity?" Mrs. Wilson asked, looking concerned.

"Uummh, yeah, I think so," I answered.

"Are you sure you don't want us to take you home, dear?"

"No, I'll be okay," I said as I clutched my churning stomach.

"You don't look okay," Mr. Wilson commented.

Then suddenly, I knew that I was *not* going to be okay.

"Where is the ladies' room?" I asked urgently.

"Right next to the concession stand," Mr. Wilson answered.

"I'll go with you, Charity," Mrs. Wilson replied.

But before she could finish talking, I was already up and running down the aisle. I just hoped that I could make it to the restroom before I got sick. Oh, no, no, . . . please, I don't want this to happen . . . it can't happen. Then I realized that I wasn't going to make it. To make matters worse, I threw up right in front of the concession stand with about sixteen zillion people staring at me.

"Oh, gross," I heard someone say. What a mess. How humiliating. Mrs. Wilson arrived and helped me to the ladies' room so I could get cleaned up.

"Don't worry about it. These things happen," she said. "I'll bet they're cleaning the floor already."

Sure enough. By the time we left the ladies' room, a maintenance person was mopping the floor. We walked back to our seats.

"I think we should get Charity home," Mrs. Wilson said to her husband.

"No. I'm feeling much better now," I said. I didn't want to ruin the rest of their afternoon. Besides, it was true, I really did. So we stayed the rest of the game. Mr. Wilson was happy when the Steelers won the game. As we walked out, Mrs. Wilson felt sorry for me and bought me a souvenir T-shirt.

When I got back to the house, I called Brittany.

"How's it going?" I asked. "Are they driving you crazy yet?"

"No, not at all," she said. "We've been having a wonderful day. We worked in the garden for a couple of hours. Then I helped your mother bake bread. And now she's been letting me help her with the scrapbook about the history of the house."

Brittany was helping with *our* scrapbook? That was our project, my mother's and mine. We'd worked on it together for a long time.

"How was the game?" she asked.

"Oh, great, really great," I bragged. "It was a fabulous game. I can't remember when I've had so much fun." For some reason I suddenly felt as if Brittany and I were competing. There was no way I was going to tell her about getting sick on junk food—not if she was having the time of her life.

"Well, I'm glad you had such a good time. I'd better go now. I'm going to read Molly her bedtime story."

"Oh," I said, "don't you know? Molly won't let anyone except my mother read to her. She just has a fit if anyone else tries."

"That's funny," she said.

"What's funny?" I asked.

"She wanted me to read to her," she replied. "She came up to me and handed me a book and said, 'night-night stowy, Bwittany.'"

"Really?" I said, feeling a little left out. "Let me tell her goodnight, okay?"

After a minute, I heard Molly yell, "Nooooo!"

"What's wrong?" I asked when Brittany came back to the phone.

"She won't talk to you," she answered.

My own sweet baby sister wouldn't talk to me?

"Oh, well, guess I'll see you at school tomorrow," I said, feeling more annoyed than ever.

"Bye," she replied cheerfully.

The next morning, Brittany was watching for me when her mother dropped me off.

"Nice shirt," she said looking at the game T-shirt.

I just smiled.

Then I noticed there was something on her hand. It looked like a big bandage.

"What happened to your hand?" I asked.

"Oh, nothing," she said. "Just a little burn."

"It's kind of a big bandage for a little burn, isn't it? How did you do that?"

"Well, when I was taking the bread out of the oven, your brother ran through the kitchen, and I guess I wasn't paying attention to what I was doing. So-oo, I accidentally burned it on the pan. But it's okay now, really."

"I'm glad, if you say so," I said. "Leave it to good old Zach."

Then I noticed that something seemed to be wrong with her legs, too.

"What happened to your legs?" I asked. They were covered with red blotches.

"Oh, they're okay. Now."

"But there are red blotches all over them."

"Oh, yeah, well, those are hives," she replied. "Who would have thought that I was allergic to ant bites? I stepped into a pile of ants while we were working in the garden and the nasty little things bit me. It's a lot better now. I had to sit in an oatmeal bath last night. But it doesn't itch much anymore." She looked hopefully at the welts on her legs.

The bell rang for first period.

"I've got to go," she said.

"See you in Mr. Boring's," I said.

It looked as if Brittany's introduction to life at my house wasn't as perfect as she'd led me to believe.

* * * * *

Boring's class was as boring as usual and then, thankfully, it was lunch time. Brittany and I walked to our regular table.

She smiled as she opened her lunch bag.

"M-m-m-m," she said, "a sandwich on freshly baked bread, crunchy vegetables right out of the garden, and homemade chocolate chip cookies."

I looked down at the school lunch plate. The spaghetti looked greasy, the broccoli was limp and over-cooked, and the brownie was small and dry. I picked up my fork and carefully prodded the lump of pasta. Finally, I picked up a slice of French bread. It was pretty tasteless, but at least it looked harmless.

"You don't look like you're enjoying that," she remarked a little sarcastically.

"We didn't have time this morning to make a lunch. Your mom is starting her new job, and she was in a hurry," I said. "So she handed me lunch money and said I'd have to buy today."

"I brought you some extra cookies," she said as she handed me some.

"You're a lifesaver," I said, and I took them from her.

Then I noticed that she was scratching her legs every couple of minutes.

"Are your hives getting worse?" I asked.

"They're just acting up a little," she said. "I'll be okay. But I think I'll see if the school nurse can give me something." She got up from the table and stood there, looking all blotched and bandaged.

"Guess I'm not exactly ready to become a professional farmer yet," she said.

"No, not yet," I agreed.

Eleven

As I walked to class, I watched Brittany limp toward the nurse's office. I guess I wasn't looking where I was going because I bumped into someone going in the door to Fine Arts.

"Sorry," I said. Then I realized this someone wasn't just anyone. It was Dave Prince. As far as I'm concerned, he is still the cutest guy in the whole school.

"Hi," he said.

"Uhmmm, er, hi," I stammered.

"I think we're heading the same way," he said, smiling.

"Yeah, uh, I think so, Fine Arts," I replied, surprised that I was capable of speech at this point.

When class started, the teacher assigned us partners. It must have been my lucky day, because I was teamed with Dave.

For the assignment, we had to listen to classical music and write down the feelings we associated with the mood of the music.

At first, I felt. pretty stupid. I could tell Dave felt funny, too. But after a few minutes, we really started to talk about the music. It was interesting. I even admitted to Dave that my parents liked to play classical music at dinnertime, a fact that I had previously admitted to no one. We ended up having a good time.

Class was over all too soon, and we walked out together.

Then Dave said, "Charity, I have a basketball game tonight, but maybe, I'll, uh, call you later." Now he was the one who was stammering.

"Sure," I answered. "See ya." I felt as if my heart had wings.

When school ended, I was still flying up somewhere in the ionosphere. Dave Prince wanted to call me. It was so cool. When I got to my new home, I ran up the stairs two at a time. I just had to call Brittany and tell her what happened.

My mom answered the phone.

"Hey, Mom."

"Hi, Honey. How you doing?" she asked.

"Fine."

"Boy, I don't know if you miss us," she said, "but, we sure miss you."

I felt a lump in my throat.

"I miss you guys, too," I said. Suddenly it didn't matter about the scrapbook or Molly or anything. We talked for a while about school in general and things at home. Then I asked to speak to Brittany.

"She's not here, hon," Mom replied. "She needed a book from the library, and your dad took her over to get it. I'll tell her to call you when she gets in."

"Okay, Mom. Guess I'll talk to you later."

I hung up. The house was quiet and empty. I settled down to do my homework. I had an assignment in almost every class, so it was going to take quite a while. I saved time on a social studies research paper on Japan by using Brittany's computer with the CD encyclopedia. We didn't have anything like that on the computer at my house. That was probably why Brittany had to go to the library. It was neat to be able to have the TV on while I typed—right in the comfort of Brittany's room. Two hours went by and I figured she was back, so I tried to call her again. This time the phone was busy.

I finished my homework. It was about six o'clock when I heard a car in the driveway and went downstairs to see who was home.

Brittany's dad stepped in the door. He was carrying a briefcase in one hand, and several cartons of take-out Chinese food in the other. I remembered Brittany saying that they only cooked on weekends. We set the breakfast bar in the kitchen with three plates. A few minutes later, Mrs. Wilson came in and sat down wearily beside us.

"You look exhausted," Mr. Wilson commented to her.

"I am," she replied. "I'd forgotten how hard it is to start a new job."

"Hope you like Chinese," Mr. Wilson said to me as he scooped some of each of the cartons on to my plate. "Sweet n' sour chicken, Szechwan, broccoli beef, fried rice, wantons and egg rolls."

"Looks good," I replied, even though the stirfry couldn't really compare to my mother's cooking.

It was a fairly quiet dinner.

Finally Mrs. Wilson said, "I talked to Brittany this afternoon. She called me at work and told me how things were going."

"I tried to call her this afternoon," I replied. "But she was at the library then, and she never called me back."

It was then that I realized that David hadn't called yet. Oh well, maybe he'd gotten busy.

As soon as we finished loading the dishwasher, I went back upstairs and called Brittany.

"Finally!" I said when she answered. "I've tried to call you all afternoon. Wait until I tell you. Guess who said he was going to call me?"

"I already know," she said. "David Prince. He called here looking for you."

"He called there? He called *you?*" I said with disbelief.

"I didn't say he called *me,*" she answered. "I said he called *here*. He didn't know your phone number, but he knew your name. So he looked up McKay in the phone book and called here."

"So did you tell him where I was?"

"Well, er, yes, eventually," she vaguely replied.

"What do you mean 'eventually'?" I asked.

"I mean, at first he just assumed that he was talking to you. And I assumed he was calling me."

"Oh, really?" I said getting slightly indignant. "Isn't that just convenient of you. I can't believe you would pretend to be me, just to talk to him."

"I wasn't pretending anything," she answered

angrily. "He just said hi and who he was and started talking. He didn't ask for you. Then later on, he started to talk about the music project that you were working on together, well, naturally I didn't know anything about it. So then he thought he had the wrong number, and I told him that he didn't. That this was your house. Then I told him all about how we'd switched and we ended up talking for a while."

"Exactly how long did you talk?"

"Oh, I don't know, maybe an hour."

"An hour! Well, how nice for you," I said sarcastically.

"You're making it sound as if I did something on purpose," she said.

"I just find it hard to believe that you could talk to someone for that long and not wonder why he was calling you."

"Oh, sorry," she said even more bitterly. "I guess I'm such an ugly troll that he couldn't possibly have been calling me. Well, good-bye, Miss America, I'd better get my beauty sleep." Then she hung up.

"Boy, what nerve!" I thought as I banged the phone down on the receiver. I was so mad. Some friend she was! How could she talk to someone for an hour and not realize that he thought she was someone else? No way. I wasn't buying it.

I took a shower and got ready for bed. Then I climbed in and switched the TV on with the remote. After a while, I turned it off and tried to sleep.

But sleep wouldn't come. I couldn't stop thinking about things. My mind was racing a hundred miles an hour. This wasn't just a switch—Brittany was ruining my life. First, it was my little brother— playing games with him, pretending to be the perfect sister so he would idolize her. Then, she takes over the scrapbook that my mother and I had been working on for years. Who knows what she did to that? Then, she makes my baby sister turn on me—fixes it so she won't even talk to me. At school, she gloats about her delicious lunch while I'm choking on gross cafeteria food. And last, but not least, she pretends to be me on the phone, just to get David. Maybe that was her plan all along.

This was not going the way I thought it would. Not at all.

Twelve

The next morning I was still angry. As I got ready for school, I looked around Brittany's room. It didn't look the same to me. It made me think of her. Everything about it annoyed me now. Her fancy furniture. Her designer everything. Her expensive stereo and TV. I felt as if everything in here was screaming, "She thinks she's better than you!"

I picked up my book bag and went downstairs. I didn't want to eat breakfast or talk to her mother or anything.

Mrs. Wilson drove me to school, remarking that I was very quiet.

"I hope everything's all right, Charity," she said as we pulled up to the school.

"I'm fine," I replied to reassure her, even if it wasn't exactly true. None of this was her fault. I didn't think it was my fault, either. It was all Brittany's.

I kept thinking about it all morning, and I knew what I had to do. By the time third period came, I didn't even want to look at Brittany. I realized that I'd have to talk to her at lunch time, whether I wanted to or not.

When the bell rang, I went into the lunchroom and sat down at our regular table. After a couple of minutes, Brittany sat down, too, but she didn't say anything. Nobody said anything, we just ate in stony silence. Finally, I couldn't stand it any longer.

"I don't want to live at your house anymore," I said.

"Well, that's good," she answered, "because I don't want to live at your house anymore, either."

"I can't stand your house, or your room, or anything in it."

"Don't worry. As soon as you get your stuff out of there, you'll never have to be in it again."

"Good," I said.

"Good," she said, and we both got up and walked in opposite directions.

David wasn't in Fine Arts class that day, and it was just as well. I didn't want to have to hear about his conversation with Brittany or anything else. I was pretty confused right now about the whole thing. I mean did David like me? Or did he like Brittany? Was

Brittany my friend? Could I be friends with someone whose life was so different from mine—or was our friendship doomed from the beginning because of it? I had more questions than I had answers.

* * * * *

After school, I couldn't wait to get my things together and get back home. Mrs. Wilson was still at work, so I had to take the school bus. As soon as I got to Brittany's, I ran up the stairs to her room. I yanked open the suitcases and stuffed in everything as fast as I could. I picked up both suitcases and hurried down the stairs. I realized then that I couldn't very well just leave without saying anything to Mr. and Mrs. Wilson. So I took out a piece of notebook paper and wrote them a note.

Dear Mr. and Mrs. Wilson,
Thank you for letting me stay at your house. I enjoyed it and you've been very nice. But things aren't working out the way I thought they would, and I've decided that I want to go back home.

Thanks,
Charity

Then I tacked the note up on the refrigerator where they couldn't miss it.

I picked up the phone and called my house. Maybe my mom could come and get me now.

"Hello?" It was Brittany. No way I was going to talk to her. I hung up without saying anything.

I was too mad to wait around—I just wanted to go, right now. I picked up the suitcases and started to walk. I underestimated the weight of the suitcases, and I had to stop occasionally to rest. None of that mattered when I got to the end of my driveway and saw my house. It never looked better.

I opened the door to the kitchen and there was my mom, looking a little worried.

"Happy to have you home, sweetheart," she said, as she held the door so I could drag the suitcases inside. "Why didn't you call me? I would have picked you up."

"Yeah, I know. Did Brittany tell you I was coming?" I asked.

"Yes, she did, Charity," my mother replied. "Brittany explained to me that you two had decided to move back to your own homes. I have to say, the big switch didn't last very long."

"Three days," I said. "Just three days."

"Is there some special reason?"

101

"Well, it just didn't turn out the way I expected it to," I answered.

"Brittany's still here," my mother said. "She's packing her things now."

I looked up the stairs toward my room, but I didn't make a move to go up there. I didn't want to see Brittany anyway. A couple of minutes later, she came down, carrying her things.

"Thank you for letting me stay here," Brittany said to my mother.

"Oh, you're very welcome," she replied. "Do you need a ride to your house?"

"No, I called my mother at work and she's coming to get me now."

I noticed Brittany's eyes looked a little red, as if she'd been crying. She picked up her suitcases and went to the door.

"I'll wait out here for her, if you don't mind," she said.

"Sure, Brittany," my mother replied. She turned toward me. "Don't you want to say good-bye?"

I simply picked up my bags and went up the stairs to my room. I couldn't say anything. When I got to my room, I looked out the window and watched Brittany walk down the driveway. She walked slowly with her shoulders slumped as if she was sad. A few

102

minutes passed, and then Brittany's mother's car pulled into the driveway. Brittany got into the car, and they pulled away.

I was still angry, but now I was sad, too. I wondered . . . had I lost a good friend?

Thirteen

The rest of the week was just awful. When I first got back home, my parents kept bugging me to try to find out what happened. At dinner, I was bombarded with questions.

"Did you have some sort of disagreement?" my father asked.

"Did you get homesick?" my mother interrogated.

"Did Brittany's parents kick you out of their house?" Zach demanded.

It was just too much.

"No!" I yelled, glaring at Zach.

"Don't be so overly sensitive," Dad remarked. "We're just all wondering what caused you to come home so soon."

"I think she's embarrassed about the whole thing," my mother commented to my father as if I wasn't even there.

"I'm not embarrassed," I said, annoyed. "Things just didn't turn out the way I expected."

"They seldom do in life," my father lectured. "You know what your grandfather used to say, 'Fish and guests both stink after three days.'"

I loved being compared to stinky fish.

"I just didn't like the way she took over everything in my life—my family, my scrapbook, my phone calls . . .," I replied.

"Oh, I see," Dad interrupted. "The old green-eyed monster."

"Green-eyed monster? Are you suggesting that I'm jealous?" I asked angrily.

"Well, it does kind of sound that way, Charity," Dad continued.

"You said that you didn't like the way she 'took over' your life. I thought that was the main objective," Mom added. "You said that you wanted to switch houses, lives, everything. Right?"

Leaning on my elbows, I glowered at my plate. I didn't like this conversation, and I wasn't going to answer any more questions.

Things were even worse at school.

I avoided Brittany all the time. At lunch, we sat at different tables. I usually wound up sitting with Heather. Most of the time, Brittany sat alone.

"Where's your friend?" Heather asked at lunch when I sat down next to her on Wednesday.

"Over there," I answered, pointing.

Heather put down the thick book she'd been reading. "Want me to ask her to sit over here with us?" she asked.

I shook my head, and said, "No way. Haven't you noticed that we haven't been sitting together all week?"

Heather sat there thinking for a minute.

"Are you guys mad at each other or something?" she asked finally.

"You mean you didn't notice till now?" I replied.

"Guess not," Heather said as she shrugged her shoulders. We ate quietly for a few minutes. Then she asked, "Did you two have some sort of disagreement?" She was beginning to sound like my father.

"Oh, brother," I said as I got up from the table. I couldn't stand it. "See you later, Heather."

Heather is really okay, but sometimes she doesn't have a clue.

Things didn't go so smoothly with David Prince either.

He finally came back to school on Thursday. He'd had the flu and that was the reason he hadn't called. I met him on the way to Fine Arts.

106

"Hi, Charity," he said.

"How are you feeling?" I asked, not knowing what else to say.

"Fine, I guess," he replied, blowing his nose into a huge wad of tissues.

He didn't look fine. His hair was a mess. It stuck up in the front as if he'd just gotten out of bed. His face looked pale, his eyes watery, and his nose red. He was definitely *not* the cutest boy in the school today.

"I tried to call you the other day and I wound up talking to Brittany," he coughed and wheezed and snorted into his tissues some more.

"Yeah, I know," I said, "but I'm back home now. Are you sure you're okay?"

He shrugged.

He smelled like vapor-rub and cough drops.

I backed up a little. Maybe he was contagious.

"See you later," I said, relieved to go to my seat.

By Friday, I had begun to wonder if Brittany and I were ever going to speak again. Then— fate entered the picture.

We were in Mr. Boring's class. He announced that we were going to have to give a presentation on our recycling project. That meant I would have to talk to Brittany whether I wanted to or not.

"Okay, class, get with your partners and plan what you are going to say. As part of the assignment, I want you to make sure your presentation answers some of the questions I've written on the board."

Reluctantly, Brittany and I stood up and pulled our desks closer together.

For a few minutes, neither of us said anything. Then Mr. Boring glared at us because we obviously were not doing the assignment.

"Okay," I sighed, "what are we going to tell the class?"

"Let's write stuff down," she answered, taking out two pieces of paper and handing one to me.

"Question number one," I read aloud from the board. "Explain the types of recycling you displayed."

"That's easy," Brittany said, and she wrote down the items we had pasted to the board.

"Question two, give three examples of how this helps the environment."

We each wrote down some reasons.

"Question number three, what did you learn from the project?"

Neither of us answered.

Finally I said, "Not to do the project at my house."

I guess that broke the ice, because we both started to giggle and then to laugh. Mr. Boring heard us laughing and glared at us again, so we quieted down.

"You know, Brittany," I explained, "I got angry because it seemed like you were doing more than just switching places with me—like you were taking over. My brother adored you. My sister let you read to her. My scrapbook. Everything in my life seemed to fit you better."

"Not really," she said. "I pretended that everything was going great all the time, but it really wasn't. I just didn't want you to know. I mean, I liked having your brother and sister around—but after a while I wished I could be alone for a few minutes. And the garden was much more work the second time, not even counting the ants attacking me. I made it sound great because you were having so much fun. I was kind of envious about not going to the football game."

"Oh, please, don't even mention the football game."

"Why?" she asked. "I thought it was the greatest thing in the world."

"No, it was probably one of the worst days of my life. I got sick. In fact, I threw up in front of about a million people."

She made a face, half-sympathetic, half-disgusted. "I didn't know," she said.

"It was my own fault. I got carried away on the junk food. I didn't want you to know because I was embarrassed."

"Sounds like we kind of did the same thing," she remarked.

"I am sorry for getting mad at you. It was really dumb," I said.

"I'm sorry, too," she replied.

"Nothing turned out the way that I thought it would."

"You're right about that."

"So where do we go from here?" I asked.

"Can we go back to being friends?" she asked.

"I hope so. I think so," I replied.

"I can if you can."

"So, question number three," she asked, "what did you learn from this?"

"I can answer that," I said. "That you don't really know what someone else's life is like until you live it."

Brittany nodded her head vigorously, "That's for sure!"

About the Author

As a child growing up in Florida, Deborah Abrahamson had an overly active imagination.

"My mother told me that I kept the neighborhood kids captivated with my stories, even when I was very young," Deborah says. "By age seven, I was writing poetry, and at age nine, I made up my own newspaper."

Though she first became a commercial artist and illustrator, Deborah never lost the love of writing. "After I had children of my own, I rediscovered children's books and knew that that was what I wanted to write."

She currently lives in Seminole, Florida, with her husband, four sports-minded children, a rabbit, a spoiled cat, and a recently adopted golden retriever. When not writing or taking care of the family, Deborah spends her time volunteering in the schools, as well as watching basketball, soccer, and little league games.